The Receiver

The Receiver

A Novella

Samara Mae

THE RECEIVER
A NOVELLA

iUniverse books may be ordered through booksellers or by contacting:

iUniverse
1663 Liberty Drive
Bloomington, IN 47403
www.iuniverse.com
844-349-9409

Because of the dynamic nature of the Internet, any web addresses or links contained in this book may have changed since publication and may no longer be valid. The views expressed in this work are solely those of the author and do not necessarily reflect the views of the publisher, and the publisher hereby disclaims any responsibility for them.

Any people depicted in stock imagery provided by Getty Images are models, and such images are being used for illustrative purposes only. Certain stock imagery © Getty Images.

ISBN: 978-1-5320-9203-9 (sc)
ISBN: 978-1-5320-9204-6 (e)

Library of Congress Control Number: 2021903911

Print information available on the last page.

iUniverse rev. date: 02/27/2021

PART I

Love is Agony

Once there was a girl
who could feel other people's pain...

And I don't mean empathy.

Every day it was someone else—another life relieved and another pain or disease to endure. But it was worth it. Yes, she would feel it, but the one whose pain she felt didn't. Even if it was only for a day, she was glad to help as much as she could.

It would start with a ripple.

Some days she woke up screaming, others crying, and some days she didn't notice a difference at all—not at first anyway. More than once, she opened her eyes to see nothing at all. She would panic at first, naturally, until realizing that it wasn't anything too detrimental. She never saw them coming. Then there were days when she felt nothing, nothing at all, and it was almost nice. Almost.

She was the Receiver, who took on someone else's pain for just twenty-four hours. Some mornings her soul felt shattered, feeling the despair of heartbreak and longing. She got used to it. She grew tired but remained strong. There were times when she couldn't get out of bed at all—many times. When she found her leg limp and aching, she knew the bestower's must have been broken. Some days she felt starved no matter how much she ate. She much preferred the disabilities; she could handle not hearing, speaking, or moving much for one day. The sicknesses were what scared her.

The bestowers knew about her, of course. They prayed and sometimes begged for a break—albeit a brief one—from their troubles. They chose a day, and she received them. All of them. Even those who didn't ask, she stole troubles from—only temporarily, of course. Whether it be for parents unwilling to see their too-young child struggle, a friend or sibling who needed to see their comatose loved one, or a significant other who couldn't bear to see their partner suffer, she accepted. She should've been called "the Reliever," but she didn't like the way it sounded.

She had always been aware of her own pain and misery, but those of *two* were difficult. She claimed they were a distraction.

"It's no way to live!" she was told.

But she only ever replied, "It's the only way I can in good conscience."

It was her choice. "The right choice," she claimed.

The other option wasn't an option: she refused to let anyone else feel *her* pain, refused to let herself be free of affliction while a different person felt it every day. So she took it. Others were not as selfless.

One day—only one—they were granted, if needed. But she was kind to a fault.

"Please, I can't take it!" they'd plead.

"I'm going to break," they'd exaggerate.

"I'm going insane," they'd lie.

But she took the pain regardless.

"Just let me do this," she'd plead.

"I can handle anything," she'd exaggerate.

"I'm fine," she'd lie.

It was a gift, or it was the way she saw it: a life not held back by illness or injury, a person given a chance to live. It was agonizingly beautiful seeing things through another's eyes, feeling what they felt, and experiencing life like them. It was something to learn from. She smiled on good days, laughed even, and had fun when she could…only to return to being alone and dying from the inside out.

Her bedroom was her cell.

But the canvas was her sanctuary.

Art was the only way she could give herself relief. So, when she had the strength, she expressed any pain inside her on a page, in a sculpture, through a paintbrush, her voice, or with just a pencil.

"Only in art am I free," she proclaimed.

Soon her room was full of her creative relentlessness. Walls covered and mind occupied—her persistence was to be admired.

But some days she could do nothing other than sit and suffer. It was unbearable to watch. She was so young, and to feel so much pain… It wasn't right. The bestowers didn't deserve her giving heart.

On rare occasions, she would sing her favorite Sara Bareilles song to herself when she thought she was alone.

"It's not simple to say, that most days, I don't recognize me…"

Music helped her to stay calm, but not when it was very quiet or very loud—that was a bad sign. Some days she sat in silence, resting her head on the nearest shoulder and breathing shallowly. For all that she went through and all she experienced, she was absolutely remarkable.

But some people just didn't care.

It was just another morning, another blind eye to turn away.

"Two sightless souls in a row; this doesn't happen often." She carried on, thinking it unimportant. "But this migraine is new."

The next day, she opened her eyes expecting cramps or the sorrow of another, but it was black. Everything was black, still. But you wouldn't know; her eyes looked as right as rain—from the outside.

Then she had a realization: "They didn't take it back." A small cry shuddered up her spine and poured out of her lips.

It wasn't the first time. One day she woke up with a pain in her toe that never went away—a bunion, of all things to receive. But this was different; this was the next tragedy of the Receiver. Not only did the bestower refuse to take back their burden, they also stole away her vision. It was a two-way street; both parties had to accept for the transfer to work.

Those greedy bastards.

For days she wept, hoping that maybe the tears would clear away the darkness. They didn't. She couldn't see her work anymore, so art was nearly pointless. It almost broke her.

But soon she was back on her feet—or in a wheelchair or crutches, depending on the day. She cooked carefully and listened to audiobooks; making the best of any situation was a superpower of hers.

After burning herself only a few times, she was even able to make scrambled eggs and bacon—with supervision. Nothing could stop her, it seemed. I almost believed it.

She never called it a curse, even if that's what it was— biting and gnawing at every bit of sanity she had. Some days she had to be locked in her room, her outbursts ceasing only because of exhaustion or satisfaction from smashing pieces of her artwork.

They were moved to a safer location after that.

Some days she didn't wake up at all; coma patients were given the day off. Other times she awoke in the middle of the night, a nervous wreck from nightmares so vivid they scared her to bits. Fear was the worst ailment, but her bravery reigned undefeated.

Until one extraordinarily dreadful day.

It was the day after her twenty-second birthday, a cool November breeze in the air. She wasn't supposed to *receive* anything on her birthday—other than gifts of love. So the next morning, her paralyzed state was somewhat expected.

"It's just the bottom half," she assured me.

It was still more than enough to need the wheelchair. If she could still see, she would've had fun rolling around her apartment, trying not to break lamps and other things. But she wouldn't dare to that day; you could say her sight was less than reliable.

She still bumped into furniture and appliances, even with help. She almost spilled water all over herself; it was nearly comical. Yet her laughter wasn't sincere.

Her ability was sometimes a mystery. The only thing to be sure of was that it wasn't always fair.

Evening came with reluctance, the sun setting bitterly behind the trees. As the night grew darker, the Receiver eventually finished her late-night snack and rolled into the kitchen, sighing a solemn breath.

Then her plate clattered onto the floor as she suddenly felt everything at once—a pain so abrupt and breathtaking that she had no time to react. If she weren't already sitting, she would've collapsed next to her plate.

An ambulance arrived and took her to the hospital with haste. It was a miracle she stayed alive for that long. Although she was clearly in great pain, her appearance remained the same: bones intact, skin untouched, and a face just as angelic as on any other day, if not slightly paler.

She knew the doctors couldn't help. No one could help—not her at least. She faded in and out of consciousness but vividly heard a rapid beeping, mutters, and shouts all yanking her back into reality. She was dying.

It was late. She looked weaker than anyone had ever seen her—weaker than anyone had ever been allowed to see her. But the pain was more than her body could handle. She heard cursing.

This pain was not her own. Whatever happened to the bestower—whether it was falling from a place too high, being hit by a car too fast, or some other tragically fatal event—she wasn't the only one about to flatline.

"Hey, angel, can you hear me?" A calm but urgent voice cooed her back to the waking world.

"Yes, beautiful." Her voice sounded as weak as she must have felt.

"Oh my god." I cupped her face in my hands. "Please don't go."

Her eyes were unfocused but they seemed to gaze into my very essence.

"Everything has its time."

"But that time doesn't have to be now!" I felt helpless, internally beating myself up for letting her have no regard for herself.

She reached out and touched my tearstained face— her hands cold as ice.

I couldn't let her go. "Just postpone your time until midnight, huh?" My voice cracked.

She shook her head, blind eyes gazing at me knowingly. "I won't last that long."

How is she already at peace with this?

For her whole life I had watched her suffer, bearing the weight of others on her shoulders—even before becoming the Receiver—never even *considering* what was good for *her* or what *she* needed. Well, I was done.

"Then give it to me. Give me your abilities."

She took both of my hands in hers; they grew colder.

"You know I won't do that."

Traditionally, the role of the Receiver is passed down through birth; however, that didn't really apply this time. But if—*if*—I could convince her, maybe I could relieve her *and* the bestower.

"I'm not asking. Give me your pain; give *me* your abilities."

It was minutes to midnight, but she was fading *fast*. I had to do something—*anything*. The person whose pain she felt was going too, and it didn't make much sense, but if I could get her to transfer her abilities to me in time—I could potentially save them both.

Now was the time to act.

"Just give me a chance," I pleaded.

"I can be just as strong as you," I exaggerated.

"I need you to stay," I cried.

The doctors couldn't explain it, but they said she likely wouldn't make it till morning. She coughed horrendously. If her body had matched her state, I imagine there would have been blood spattered on the bland, sterile hospital sheets.

"I couldn't," she sputtered out, stubborn even while dying. "And it's not my pain to give."

I cradled her face, desperately trying to reach her. "Listen to me; this is your only shot at surviving—at living a *normal* life. Have you never wanted that?!"

Just keep her alive, just keep her—

"I don't *need* normal; I need *you*: happy and stable." A small but warm smile broke through on her pained face.

This is it. Now or never. "What about the person out there who's also dying? You know that if you make me the Receiver—give me your abilities—before the next pain comes tomorrow, we could save *both of you*."

This isn't going to work. I was reduced to an ugly sob.

Her face showed guilt, sorrow, and, most prominently, fear. I knew that look; it was the same look that I had on whenever she was in great pain or felt such misery. I knew that look all too well.

I gently stroked her languid hair and slipped it behind her ear. "You deserve a chance at happiness too. Angel, please, let someone help *you* for once." Her cheeks were frigid under my burning tears.

11:59. Oh god.

I moved in close as a desperate last attempt to save her life. Pressing my trembling lips against hers, I kissed with all the passion of the words I wished I had time to say. She loosely held my forearms and replied with soft affection, almost thanking me for staying with her for all that time. As we parted with nostalgia, I felt a shiver go up my spine.

"I love you, beautiful" she whispered.

A feeling of peace passed through us both.

"I love you too, angel."

I gazed down at the serene face of the former Receiver, going numb when an eerie beeping turned into a drone.

12:00 a.m. November 9th—the end of the most precious life that ever was.

❣

As months passed, our apartment became lonely—it and me. We witnessed all her ups and downs together: her good days, her not-so-good days, her worse days…it's not something you just get over.

Some say an artist's work is more valuable after their passing, but I wouldn't—I *couldn't*—sell her art for the world. They may break my heart a little more each time I look at them, but—as pieces of her, reminders of her—they make me feel better too.

I can't let go.

And I need all the help I can get after taking over the role of the Receiver. I won't lie; it's tough work.

I found the bestower who was relieved of his lower-body paralysis…just to be hit by a car and put back in a wheelchair that day. *That's what you get for not looking both ways.*

He did survive, though, and I suppose that's worth something. He seems like a much more appreciative person now. Once he heals enough, he can finally give those legs a proper go. My girlfriend took his permanent immobility with her. *That lucky bastard.*

Resentment aside, I got a fresh start. It's not the best start, but it's a fresh one. No one ever said life was meant to be easy—quitting is easy. And when you have the pain of two souls on your back, it's even more difficult.

I discovered that some of her methods of relaxation are quite useful. I often do origami, read, and even write a bit on my less "stressful" days. But the most therapeutic activity for me is singing.

I often find myself reminiscing over a song she used to unknowingly serenade me with. I can't help but feel connected by it, although it's hard to sing it without tearing up.

> *"She's imperfect, but she tries*
> *She is good, but she lies*
> *She is hard on herself*
> *She is broken and won't ask for help*
> *She is messy, but she's kind*
> *She is lonely most of the time*
> *She is all of this mixed up and baked in a beautiful pie*
> *She is gone, but she used to be mine…"*

My angel. She was wrong about one thing: borrowed misery is terrible at diverting attention. Nothing can distract me from missing her.

Now I'm the girl who ~~can~~ chooses to feel other people's pain as the Receiver.

And I can only dream of living up to the legacy.

PART II

Love is Bittersweet

About one year earlier (through angel eyes)…

A knock on the door.

Who could that be?

I tossed my sketchbook aside and hesitantly got up from my sunken spot on the couch. Then the sound of jingling keys made me pause. The door swung open.

"Surprise!" My roommate beamed at me with a bouquet of roses in her hands.

I shook my head and laughed. "I thought you were a burglar."

She shut the door and turned around, wrapping me in her arms.

"I am! *The* burglar, that is." She giggled, pulling away and displaying the gorgeous flowers to me. "These are for you, angel."

I took them with gratitude. "Thank you, beautiful; they're lovely." I smiled; I couldn't stop smiling.

She hung her coat by the door. "Like you."

I rolled my eyes, burying my nose in the fresh blossoms. *Wasting money on me.* "Why are you back so soon?"

"Class was canceled. Professor had a family emergency, and the TAs didn't know what to do." She chuckled.

"That's…" I wasn't sure if I should say "awesome" or "awful," so I said, "Wow."

"Yep." She smiled at me, taking the bouquet from my hands and setting it on the coffee table as she leaned in close. "So I stopped by the store on my way home…and you know the rest."

"Do you wanna watch TV? *Say Yes to the Dress* is on…" I persuasively crooned in her ear.

"It is?" She perked up. "What are we waiting for then?" She pulled me by the arm and plopped next to my spot on the couch.

I grinned. "Works every time."

She snuggled up against me. "Any chance to hang with my gal-pal." She winked as I put my arm around her.

Things were not so sweet two and a half years ago.

It was the day after my graduation party. High school was over with, and I was finally ready to tell my parents the truth—the truth about me.

Staying in the closet for so long wasn't easy: trying to hide my cringe every time they asked if I found a boyfriend yet, stifling my laugh whenever someone asked me to be straight with them… But it was necessary.

Being a millennial in a very strict, Christian, *Republican* family was a nightmare. Sometimes I just wanted to scream. But I was the good little girl they wanted me to be—until I told them I was gay.

I probably should've waited a little longer, but I thought I was going to explode. Luckily, I was planning on moving anyway, because that was when they kicked me out.

My dad practically pushed me out the door, my suitcase flying after me. But that wasn't nearly as painful as my mother's reaction: she wouldn't even look at me.

I only had one place to go, and she was prepared.

"The bed's all made, and my mom is making dinner. Do you want me to sleep in here with you tonight, or is being next door enough?"

She always called *me* the kind one, the selfless angel who would do anything for anyone. But I know she'd drop everything for a friend, even if she didn't need to; she *wanted* to help.

"I-I think I'll be okay," I shakily replied.

She saw my pained expression and hugged me close. "Yes, you will be. And I'll be here the whole time, okay?"

My best friend—she always knew what to say.

"And I'm sure your parents will come around eventually." She was so optimistic. "My momma took some time to understand me. Hell, my sister still doesn't. But no matter what happens, I'm here."

Her family has always welcomed me and accepted me as I am. I'm forever grateful. She let me stay in her sister's old room until we went off to college a few months later.

That's why we both got jobs at the party store: to raise money for an apartment. She would walk around helping customers, restocking, and reorganizing the shelves while I worked behind the counter. Sometimes I'd catch her looking at me from across the store, or she'd try on part of a costume and make silly faces at me. I would just smile and roll my eyes.

She always knows how to cheer me up.

I gazed down at her glowing face while we laid on the couch together. *My hero.*

She noticed and smiled back up at me. "Hey, angel." She booped my nose.

I half smiled back, sighing softly before I returned my attention to the girl struggling to find her perfect dress on the screen. *I wonder if that'll be us someday.*

Then something dawned on me. "Don't you have a paper to write?"

My girlfriend answered by crinkling her nose in disgust.

"Babe, you should really get on that." *Ugh, responsibilities.*

A wild grin sprouted on her face. "I know something else I could get on."

I couldn't help but giggle as I shoved her off the couch. "Later. Paper first!"

She groaned, disappointed.

"Yeah, I know, me too." Cuddling would have to wait.

Besides being the gay cousin in a very conservative family, the first two decades of my life had been relatively normal. I only wish my family had been as accepting as my pretty damn bisexual girlfriend's. But they're my real family, I know that now.

"Babe, wake up."

I turned over and shoved my face into the pillow. "No."

I heard her giggle and felt a tug on the blankets.

I growled, "If you pull those away from me, I swear to God…"

Suddenly I felt a soft arm wrap around my waist and a light kiss placed in my hair.

"Do you even know what day it is, angel?" She posed sweetly.

I turned my head to see her right at my nose. "Saturday? The day you normally don't budge until noon?"

She grinned. "Well, yes… But it's also your birthday!"

I blinked. "It is?"

How could I forget that??

She kissed my forehead, chuckling. "Don't worry; I've already got breakfast covered."

Ah, November 7th: the big twenty-one. *Holy crap.*

Turns out she already had the whole day planned: a fancy waffle breakfast, a replanning of my "life goals," and a fun outing to a bar with our friends that evening. I was excited, but there was also something nagging at me.

Breakfast was perfect; she always had a knack for cooking, even if she didn't do it often.

I wrapped my arms around her from behind and rested my chin on her shoulder, sighing contently. "You're beautiful."

She giggled as she extracted my brunch from the waffle iron and set it on my plate. "So are you." She smiled and kissed my cheek.

It was a perfect morning.

While I dug into my golden Belgian waffle, she quickly jotted something down in a notebook. I read the words "Bucket List" in her best chicken scratch and giggled.

"Really?" I raised an eyebrow at her.

She looked at me sternly. "Do I look like I'm kidding? You're twenty-one; you get to do exciting things now!"

I nitpicked, "Technically I'm not twenty-one until seven twenty tonight." I sighed at her exasperated expression. "Alright, fine." I pondered things I'd like to do while chewing on some home-cooked bacon. "I want to see the Grand Canyon," I decidedly stated.

She smiled, writing it down as number one on the list. "What else?"

"Oh! How about going to the opera?" She grimaced slightly. "Just once?" I persuaded.

She shook her head, writing it down anyway.

I started getting bolder. "Let's see: pet a moose, hug the pope... Didn't you want to go wheelchair racing?"

She giggled. "Slow down! And yes; I'm going to beat you."

I laughed. "You wish."

We continued bantering until we decided the list was complete for now; we could always add on later.

She put it in a safe place while I cleaned up her mess in the kitchen. *Worth it.*

Hours later, we were dressed and prepped to go out. I could feel a blush grow on my cheeks as she stepped out in a shimmery purple cocktail dress. *She's beautiful.*

"Ready to go, angel?" I watched as she threw on a jacket and grabbed her keys. She was the designated driver, after all.

I swallowed nervously. "As ready as I'll ever be."

We picked up a couple of friends on the way to some popular bar in the area. I was anxious…that is, until I noticed what *kind* of bar my girlfriend had picked out.

Why am I not surprised?

"Leave it to her to find the only gay bar within a five-hundred-mile radius." We laughed while approaching the fabulously named Unicorn: Bar & Hangout.

Sitting in the unique, colorfully decorated establishment, I felt at home. I could tell my girlfriend felt the same way: we were welcome.

I could also see her eyeing a strawberry margarita across the bar. She pouted at me. She was only the designated driver because she was underage. So instead she ordered a Shirley Temple and a side of fries.

Suddenly the squad was staring at me, including the spunky bartender named Filipé.

"Uh…I'll have…some water?"

They groaned.

To my dismay and relief, my girlfriend jumped in with an unexpected request: "She'll have some hard cider with a spritz of tequila please."

I watched in mild terror as Filipé smiled and replied as if those were real words she had just said. "One Cannonball, coming up."

I hope she knows what she's doing.

When our drinks were ready, I was—again—the center of attention. They wanted me to take the first sip.

I looked at my watch, anxious. "Come on, guys, I don't even turn twenty-one for another fifteen minutes." I was answered with more groaning. "Okay, okay...but if I get in trouble for this, I'm taking you all down with me—you too, Filipé." He put his hands up in surrender.

The first sip was sort of like really strong apple juice, but then the tequila kicked in. I pursed my lips at the sourness. *Mm, that sure is...something.*

My girlfriend touched my arm, and I suddenly felt concerned, but I couldn't place why.

I gulped down the feeling and another sip, putting on a smile for my friends. "That was...great! Hit me right in the gullet. That's what's supposed to happen, right?" *I don't sound like a total idiot, right?*

Filipé nodded. *Phew.*

The girls cheered. I was officially, and a little anti-climactically, no longer an "alcohol virgin." *Woohoo.*

After the rest of that drink, and two—or three—more later, my head was spinning. I tried leaning on my also intoxicated friends for support, but I think that just made it worse. My girlfriend tried to make sure we had enough water because we were all dehydrated, and I even munched on some of her fries, but I guess I'm a lightweight. *Fantastic.*

Before I knew it, everyone was singing me "Happy Birthday." But it was all too loud, all too much—

Why are there so many colors?

—until it all faded away as I blacked out.

The next morning, I woke up with a lingering memory of my ears ringing and the feeling of my insides becoming outsides.

I figured my beautiful, magical, responsible girlfriend must have gotten us all home safe last night, based on the fact that I had ended up in my bed with no memory of getting there. *Did she carry me?*

The shutters were closed as to not let the light in and bother my hangover, but my head still felt like a brick on a stick. I also had a strange itch on my left arm that hadn't been there before, but there was no visible source of irritation. And after my girlfriend came to check on me and enlighten me as to what had happened, she stubbed her toe, and I could've sworn that I hit mine at the same time. But I was so disoriented, who could tell?

So I went on with my day and ate some soup we had in the cupboard—since soup is obviously the cure for all ailments—and watched a marathon of *Say Yes to the Dress*, since I didn't have anything better to do.

But I felt even weirder the next day: my back hurt, I could barely read the textbooks in front of me, and I had this weird, underlying sense of worry. I talked to my girlfriend about it, and she had no good explanation either—but said she was just as worried. She kept suggesting that we call my regular doctor since I was "clearly overdue for a checkup," but I convinced her to wait—until I was suddenly clenching my stomach and curled up on the floor, mumbling, "I'm fine. I'm fine…"

"Blood tests? X-rays? Is there anything that'll help us understand what's happening?" My girlfriend interrogated the nurse filling out our paperwork.

He looked up quizzically. "Sorry hon, you'll have to ask the doc; I'm just here for the lollipops."

We watched in confusion as he popped the candy into his mouth and left the room.

"Babe, relax," I assured her. "I'm sure we'll figure this out."

She huffed and crossed her arms.

I tried to tell her that she didn't have to come, but she insisted. And to be honest, I was glad to have her with me, because no matter what was going on, I knew she'd support me in any way she could.

Soon my doctor arrived, entering with all the poise and grace of a giraffe on roller skates. In fact, as soon as she opened the door, it looked as if she was the one who needed a doctor.

After almost tripping over the scale by the door and catching herself on the counter, she remarked, "Goodness, quite an entrance that was." She took off her seemingly unhelpful glasses, furrowing her eyebrows at them. "That's peculiar."

Then I think she sat on the stool in front of me, but it was hard to tell, seeing as how my eyes had suddenly become quite blurry.

I tried not to panic as I explained my unusual predicament. Though, it was a little difficult to focus with my newly impaired eyesight. The doctor took notice of this when she shone a light in my eyes.

"Hmm," she mused, turning the flashlight off. "Now, I might be going out on a limb here, but"—the doctor paused—"try these." She placed a pair of delicate glasses on my nose.

I blinked and suddenly everything became clear. "Holy crap." Then I turned to stare at my girlfriend's beautiful and befuddled face.

"Okay, is *somebody* gonna tell me what the hell is going on here?" she spouted.

The doctor sat back on her stool and took a breath. "Your symptoms…"

"Yes…?" I leaned forward in anticipation.

"…are not your own," she vaguely concluded.

My girlfriend sighed, exasperated. "Okay, you're gonna have to do better than that."

The doctor gave a small smile. "I've seen this before; you could say it's hereditary. I recommend that you speak to someone more knowledgeable in this area. I don't suppose your mother would be available—"

"No. No, she's not," I stated firmly.

She nodded. "Your grandmother then. Ruth will know."

My girlfriend and I shared a look, both perplexed.

"I'm sorry, ladies." The doctor shrugged apologetically, collecting her things. "That's the best I can do for you."

What? But she barely did anything! I hope she's not going to charge me for this.

I smiled anyway. "Well, thank you, I'll let you know what we come up with." *Not.*

"What was *that* all about?" My girlfriend exclaimed once we got in the car, my eyesight now back to normal.

"I wish I knew," I sighed, defeatedly sinking into the passenger seat.

"Well then, we'll just have to pay your grandmother a visit." A devious grin grew on her face. "I hope she likes lollipops." Then she dumped all the suckers that were in her purse onto my lap.

I couldn't help but crack up, immediately feeling better. *That's my girlfriend.*

"When did your grandma get a motorcycle?"

We stared in bewilderment at the two-seat Harley-Davidson in front of my grandmother's porch. But we were even more baffled when a stubbled biker exited through the front door and rode away on it.

Am I missing something?

I hesitantly rang the doorbell, awaiting a hug I knew would be too tight.

After a moment, my girlfriend leaned in and whispered, "Did she know we were coming?"

I blinked. "She should have. Didn't you call?"

She pulled away. "I thought you called…"

Oops.

As if on cue, my pink-cheeked grandmother opened the door. "Girls!" she exclaimed with a smile. "What a pleasant surprise."

Unlike my parents, she's always been open-minded and unconditionally loving. We became a lot closer after I left home.

"I hope you weren't busy," I started. "We meant to call…"

"Oh, don't be silly, I always have time for my two favorite ladies." She smiled, squeezing our shoulders and ushering us inside to the living room.

My girlfriend chuckled. "That's good—that we weren't *interrupting* anything."

My grandma looked mildly embarrassed. "Oh dear, you saw that, did you?" We nodded, settling onto the couch with her. "Well, I guess the cat's out. That was Jeffrey; he takes me out for rides sometimes." She flipped her hair as if to show her internal youth.

I shook my head in amusement. *Wow.*

Her face became more solemn. "I'm not getting any younger, you know. Besides, ever since your grandfather passed…"

I patted her hand. "I understand."

My girlfriend offered a gentle grin. "Good for you."

Grandma Ruth suddenly stood and closed a closet door I hadn't noticed was open—but not before I caught a glimpse of a slightly worn leather jacket.

"I don't suppose you came up just to discuss my love life, hm?" she mused.

I scratched my head. *Where do I start?*

"A *legend?* Awesome, I think," my girlfriend began. "Well, not for you."

I sighed.

"Yes, well, being the Receiver comes with a lot of responsibility. It also kind of sucks."

Well said, Grandma.

"So, you're saying that you—*and* Mom—both went through the same thing and never told me?"

She shrugged, leaning back in her seat. "I mistakenly assumed your mother would have explained it to you... We don't talk about it a lot, for obvious reasons."

I tried to wrap my head around it. I mean, this was nuts. My mom? *Her mom?* And why had I never heard of it before?

"You see, dear, your mother wasn't quite as kindhearted as I had hoped. She was entitled to her decision, but..." Grandma closed her eyes for a moment, as if she was disappointed.

"But what? What happened?" my girlfriend asked, on the edge of her seat.

"When Helen turned twenty-one, within the first week of becoming the new Receiver, she had to make a choice. She could either take someone else's pain every day...or she could give her own burdens to a different person every day." She paused.

"And she chose the latter," I concluded.

Ruth nodded. "I'm afraid so."

"So, what? Now *I* have to choose?"

"Yes, dear, and I'm sorry. It's a heavy weight to bear, but I know you'll make the right decision."

I cringed. "What did you do?"

"Take a wild guess." She gave a teasing smile.

"Right, well, I'm not sure if I can be as brave as you."

My girlfriend took my hand in hers.

Grandma shook her head. "Of course you can, but it's up to you whether you think you can handle it. Why don't you take some time to think? But not too long, mind you. After seven days from your birthday, rumor has it, the choice is made for you."

My girlfriend squeezed my hand, sensing my fear.

At least I know I'll always have her by my side.

Grandma Ruth sent us off with some homemade chocolate chip cookies and a warm smile. She told me to call if I had any more questions.

Oh, I definitely will.

I sat shotgun in my girlfriend's car and traced her profile in my head.

She thought out loud, "I guess that explains the weird things that have been happening to you whenever you get near people with physical issues, yeah? Maybe until you decide it's all sort of sporadic and uncontrollable. Good thing I'm driving, huh?"

I smiled to myself. "Yeah, good thing."

But she could tell I was worried. "Hey, it's okay, angel. We're gonna figure this out. One step at a time." She smiled reassuringly, handing me one of Grandma's cookies.

I took it. "Right. One step at a time," I repeated, less than sure.

There's still one thing that doesn't add up.

She continued, "So what? This thing is hereditary?" I nodded. "Well, I don't think that's gonna be a problem here." She laughed awkwardly, starting the car.

I didn't laugh. "But how does it work? Do I just say, 'I choose to take on others' pain and become the Receiver,' or what?"

Without missing a beat, I gasped as a shiver went up my spine and down my limbs—not a chill, exactly, but more of an awakening. And then I knew. *This is who I'm meant to be.*

My girlfriend gawked at me, noticing my distress. "Is that...*it?* Are you okay?"

I nodded, staring out the windshield. "I think so, to both."

Her grip tightened on the wheel. "Okay."

"Can we go home?" I buckled my seat belt with shaky hands.

She looked straight ahead, nodding. "Yep."

And we were off.

I was watching the scenery outside my window, attempting to relax on our way back to the apartment, when I recognized the somber notes of a piano. My girlfriend smiled and turned up the radio.

> *"That these shoes and this apron*
> *That place and its patrons*
> *Have taken more than I gave them..."*

I joined in to sing "She Used to Be Mine" by Sara Bareilles—a song that I never knew I would relate to so much in the future.

"It's not easy to know
I'm not anything like I used to be, although it's true
I was never attention's sweet center
I still remember that girl..."

For better or worse, I am the Receiver.

And I guess it's my turn to continue the legacy...but not on my own.

PART III

Love is Patience

Present-day (back to the beautiful)...

My world is empty.

A year has passed, and I am still without her. But life goes on; I make do, bitterly.

I visit her every day—well, I did. Now it tends to be every few days, or once a week when I'm too busy with work or school.

I don't know which is more painful: an actual grave or her lifeless body on the hospital bed, monitor faintly beeping in the background. She's been in a coma for what feels like an eternity. No one dares to pull the plug. I'd cut their hands off myself.

Her parents can't let her go either. They sent me a card after...the incident. I tossed it out without reading it. *The nerve.* I see them sometimes on weekends, crying, giving her their long-overdue apologies. They avoid eye contact with me when we cross paths. *As they should.*

I like to sit next to her and read stories of other empowering women like herself. Poems too. Sometimes I sing quietly, and I swear I see her smile. One of my favorite poems to read her is "Do Not Go Gentle into That Good Night." I like to think it keeps her fighting. I know that she can hear me, even though some doctors say it's impossible. No one should ever underestimate a coma patient's perception. I tell her about crazy things on the news, all the good memes, trends, whenever a new iPhone comes out, et cetera. I also rant a bit about how angry I am with the patriarchy. She's a really great listener.

Many times I've considered switching places with her—receiving her ailment so that she could live for a day. Maybe she could write me little notes, visit a friend, or even have brunch at our favorite little café. But I can never bring myself to do it. I don't think it's what she would want—to see me comatose in her place: it would hurt too much. It's probably better that she doesn't know what she's missing. I reckon it wouldn't go over too well with the hospital staff either.

This morning I stumbled upon her sketchbook. There were sketches of me, doodles of roses, even drawings of me with flowers in my hair from when we would make flower crowns together. God, she was so talented...sorry...*is*—is talented.

It was at that moment, while looking at a charcoal drawing of our hands clasped together, that I realized if—I mean *when*—she wakes up... When she wakes up, her blindness will be gone and she should be able to see her art again. Her eyes could see me again.

I had to close the book so my tears wouldn't ruin the picture.

I guess it's just one of those things where you think you're done, you think the crying's over...and then one thing, one silly little memory, is triggered by something. And then the tears just fall. It sucks.

Anyway, I miss her all the time. I had to pick up more hours at the party store and a part-time job at a coffee shop so I could pay her half of the rent. Of course, I can't always make it to work because of the stupid curse

I decided to take on. But I have my mom and friends who help, even if they don't understand the whole situation.

The only one I told everything to was my best friend—my *other* best friend. She visits me from New York sometimes and shows me her modeling portfolio. I'm really excited for her, despite my monotonous tone. I guess I'm just jealous; there's nothing stopping her. I always planned to travel more, but with my girlfriend. Now I'm worried that if I leave town…she might not be here when I get back.

My main focus has been on finally graduating and preparing to enter the real world…without her. After taking a gap year to work and take in everything that's happened, I've almost completed my double major in English and political science; she would be proud. I also already published a small collection of poems I started when I was sixteen. Good to know my emotions can get me something besides tears and broken pencils. Ha.

I'm working on a couple of okay novels right now; they're missing *depth*. That's why I need to travel, meet new people—really see the world. But that costs money and time, and I have neither. I'm trying, though; I have a jar of savings that I do my best not to touch. I've also sold some of my less sentimental drawings; I'm fairly proud of them. However, I don't have my girlfriend's patience or natural talent.

I like stories. They're personal and comforting—but at the same time exhilarating and view-changing. Words can be so powerful sometimes, and so obnoxiously meaningless other times. What's the point of writing if you're not pouring your very heart and soul into it? My angel was my muse, and without her to bounce ideas off of, to gain inspiration from…I'm lacking an anchor. I'm missing the fundamental clarity and truth that would make my work feel whole.

I hate writing.

I also love it, but my girlfriend would rather read. So even though I don't get her feedback anymore, I still read her my writing, even if it's not my best. I mean, she's kind of a captive audience, so…

Lately, my unique situation has been pretty low-key—you know, no near-death experiences (knock on wood). Some vertigo here, a few stomachaches there (I chose the wrong day to eat pizza *and* ice cream), and a few sprains every now and then. Those were embarrassing falls. Maybe it's just me, but I can't help but keep waiting for the other shoe to drop.

My girlfriend could probably answer some of my questions.

I visited Grandma Ruth a few weeks back. She's heartbroken over the whole thing, but she still treats me as part of the family and we chat on the phone sometimes. I was hoping she would have some answers for me. How come my experience as the Receiver isn't as bad as my girlfriend's was? If I don't have kids, will the cycle just stop? How did it start? And why can't I find anything at the library? How do the bestowers know? You know? It sucks not knowing.

Ruth knew some of the answers, at least.

She thought that maybe since I wasn't born into the role, that's why it's not so debilitating. That, and maybe, just maybe, I might have a higher tolerance for the pain. I can't help but feel guilty about it, even though I know it's stupid.

She figured it would probably end if I didn't pass it on somehow, which is good, I think. No one should have to go through this unwillingly, it's not fair. But it is a big deal—being the last of a legend going back…who knows how long—or at least, it feels like a big deal. She didn't seem too broken up about it though.

She doesn't know how it started. Her grandfather before her had strange aches and ailments, so he told his family stories of the legend of the Receiver. She didn't believe him until it happened to her, the firstborn.

She also said libraries are stupid and that she's banned from them now. *All of them?* I didn't ask why.

But she did say that the bestowers are guided to the Receiver by the universe—like some mystical fate. That's when I noticed the empty wine bottle.

So who *really* knows? I sure don't.

Today my good hearing was traded. Everything is off; it's like when your ears get blocked on a plane and you're walking through the airport, pulling on your lobes like a weirdo. I'm more annoyed than anything. Thank god it's Sunday, so I don't have to leave the apartment.

My mom tried to call me a few times. You can imagine how frustrating that was. I texted her that I was at the library. It worked. It also reminded me that I have to finish a French assignment and the book I'm using is overdue. Shit.

I grab my book bag and a jacket and catch a bus heading down to the campus library. There are some kids spread out here and there, probably studying or goofing around online—it's surprisingly hard to tell which.

I sneak past the front desk—which is empty, so there's not much point—and find a comfy spot near the back. I'm lucky my professor is pretty easygoing, because translating French lit is hard. We're reading a cute short story, I think, and I'm supposed to analyze the overarching theme, which is—probably—forgiveness.

But, like I said, it's hard. It must be more than that; I mean, the antagonists are hardly worth forgiving to me. I guess it's a matter of perspective.

I end up scribbling a bullshitted page of vague thoughtfulness. I'd rather not spend more time here than I have to; the librarian scares me. But as I walk through the aisles on my way out, a bright pink blur stands out from the corner of my eye. I turn to see a book with white lettering. It's called *When We Rise*. Now it's got my attention.

I anxiously pull it from the shelf, still hearing nothing but my heartbeat. I stare at the cover in awe: a kid with wild curls and glasses stands in front of a vast audience. *Cleve Jones*. I read the description on the inside cover, anticipation and a smile growing.

Where has this book been all my life?

I place it on the front desk with purpose while slyly slipping my French book through the return slot. I meet the rising librarian with an innocent smile.

So that's where she was hiding.

"I'd like to check this out please," I state while placing my card next to it.

She nods in slow approval and stamps the book with attitude.

"Be punctual," her lips command.

I squint briefly and nod once I interpret her lips. Then I *book* it out of there.

I make as much noise as I can the next morning, so grateful to hear every raucous sound. My neighbor eventually stops by to see if I'm okay. I quiet down after that. I even call my sister just to hear her obnoxious voice, and I almost wish I didn't. But, although she's not quite as open-minded as I'd like, at least she didn't abandon me.

After limping out of my first class (my entire right leg is numb), I find a bench and eagerly pull out my new book.

It pulls me into the toil and struggle of a young gay boy trying to survive in the 1970s. This was especially difficult for him because his father believed homosexuality was an illness and kept trying to "cure" him. My girlfriend's parents kicked her out, but at least they never tried to torture her. I would run away to San Francisco too if I were this kid. Then things changed, people grew, and the father recognized how important identity was to his son.

My coming out wasn't nearly as dramatic. But my sister and I did have a nice, emotional hug once she got over the differences, because I was still her sister—the same person she'd known her whole life. My eyes start to water as I read.

I kill an hour and a half, enamored by the true story, and am almost late to French Literature. I stand up with a new sense of purpose brewing inside me—and nearly fall right over.

Stupid leg.

A few friends ask me what happened, so I say it just fell asleep. There's a lot of lying as the Receiver, but it's necessary if you don't want to seem like a whack job. So I limp—ever so casually—along to my lit class.

Lying is the easy part; it's the loneliness that hurts. I don't have anyone to really open up to like my girlfriend did, to support me like I supported her. Sometimes I just have to ask myself: what would my angel do? Probably stay in bed, but I can't afford that with my tuition; though I have no way of really knowing. It probably sounds dumb, but it's as if part of my soul is missing.

I snap my head up after hearing my name, an empty silence hanging in the air.

Crap, I zoned out.

"I'll ask again. Does our protagonist simply pity the villains, or does he truly forgive them?" The professor looks at me inquisitively, as if I were actually paying attention the whole time.

I almost panic, wondering if I should cop-out or just read from my paper. But then I think about Cleve Jones and his ignorant father—who was just like my girlfriend's parents: afraid of what they didn't understand. Realization dawns on me.

The air seems to still around my desk. I hear deep sighs and muffled snores from disinterested students. I feel the mild strain of glaring ceiling lights, a heavy expectation holding me in the stiff plastic seat, waiting for a necessary conclusion.

I inhale. "At first I was angry—while reading that scene; how could anyone forgive such intolerance of diversity? But now, from the protagonist's perspective, it makes sense why someone would want to be rid of all that rage. No one likes to swallow their pride; it's a thousand times easier to stay stubborn and hold on to that grudge. It's just…not healthy.

"Yes they were ignorant, and lashed out in the worst way possible, but that was then. That was when they were afraid and defensive, trying to protect the only world that they knew. Then they learned and grew…and they were extremely brave to ask for forgiveness. I think…the most important lesson you can take from this novel…is how powerful love can be."

A few students roll their eyes. "No, stay with me on this. It's about choice. The protagonist chooses to let go of that negativity and let love into his heart. And showing compassion toward someone who's done you wrong not only teaches the wrongdoer a better way...but it also teaches the person forgiving that love is stronger than bitterness and that everyone deserves a second chance if they're willing to put in the effort.

"And—whether the wrongdoer has earned it yet or not—it provides solace, and maybe even an opportunity to forgive oneself for letting that resentment overpower them. As Wonder Woman was taught by her partner, Steve Trevor, 'It's not about deserve... It's about what you believe.'" *And my partner would want me to choose love too.* I exhale, half expecting the room to ring out in applause, but this is real life.

The professor is smiling, a faint twinkle in his eye. "Very well said. I think that about covers it." He glances around the room. "*Non?*"

I'm beaming with a new sense of self, surprised at the tear that's made its way down my cheek. *I know what I need to do.*

It's Wednesday night: the perfect time to dig into some sad memories and dust off old feelings—especially when I can't feel anything. (The bestower's hands must've been burned, leaving the nerve receptors inactive, meaning: I can't feel shit.) I'm sifting through boxes stuffed under our bed, looking for the one I buried as deep as possible. I heave the nostalgia out from beneath my grudge, taking a moment to stare it back down to size.

I open the small keepsake box. On top are the love letters I wrote to my girlfriend when we were in high school, urging her to keep going. Her years as an upperclassman were really hard; she couldn't wait to get out. I guess the letters helped her hold on.

Next are the platinum rings she wanted us to wear, but I gratefully declined. I didn't need a flimsy ring to keep a promise. *We* didn't.

I finally find what I'm looking for: a graduation photo. In it, she wears a smile, but I was the only one who knew what was really behind it. My hand is around her shoulder reassuringly, my other fist in the air. Her parents stand proudly right behind her, and my mom next to me. Except her parents aren't actually there, because we cut them out of the photo after they cut her out of their life.

My girlfriend kept the other piece, just in case. Now I'm grateful for it; maybe there is hope. I leave the open box exposed next to my dresser and set the photo pieces on my nightstand.

I used to blame her parents for what happened to her. I thought that maybe if they had never shut her out, then she would've fought harder—would've held on just a little longer. It was only natural to point a finger at them or the others that gave their pain to her, even if it was pointless.

But now I have a plan, and a new book to read her. Maybe this time I'll relieve some of my own pain. And maybe even theirs. It's what she would want.

After days of apprehension brewing inside me, Saturday finally arrives. Luckily, today's burden is only a moderate burning sensation in my chest: might be my heart, might be the anxiety—no idea. Anyway, I know her parents are going to be here at 4:30 p.m. on the dot. They may be conservative, but at least they're punctual.

My mom said I was doing the right thing, even if she couldn't resolve things with *her* family. I'm hesitantly hopeful that I can get through to them—and maybe, eventually, even forgive them.

But, honestly, I have no idea what to expect. I'm sure they're sorry, but do they hold anything against me? They don't exactly know what happened. Can't say I exactly know either. But I should end this; it's the only way to move forward. I'm choosing a life of compassion.

So I'm a little nervous. Sue me.

I spend the first couple hours of my visit pouring my emotions out to her: the book, my lit class, my revelation— it's a lot to express. Occasionally one of the nurses passes through the hallway. I'm sure they're used to this by now, but I hope they don't think that I'm completely insane.

"I mean, am I crazy? I'm no Cleve Jones—not nearly mature enough. Am I even capable of letting go? You know me; I'm spiteful. Ugh, I wish you were awake to knock some sense into me." I stop pacing and sit in the chair next to her gently breathing but otherwise still body.

Her soft, sleeping expression grounds me slightly.

"Guess I have to do everything myself." I look at her with a smirk; she doesn't answer.

I sigh. *She would've laughed at that.*

My eyes flicker open and see *When We Rise* sitting on the table beside me. My phone is buzzing. *4:30! I must've dozed off. Shit.*

My head bounces up too fast, and my vision spins a little bit until finally settling on a pair of faces making their way around the corner. I hide behind a curtain. Part of me wishes they guarded the coma ward better.

I drink in a much-needed breath and close my eyes. *You can do this; she's counting on you. Besides, you have the element of surprise.* I breathe out and open my eyes. *Here goes nothing.*

I step out from behind the curtain and meet two very stunned pairs of eyes. "Helen, Frank..." Fear grips my chest. "Hi." I shake it off. "Please, sit down." I motion to two empty chairs across from the bed and smile meekly at their bewildered faces.

An invisible flame chars away at my rib cage, as if exposing internal organs—the most vulnerable parts of me. *This was a lot easier in front of the mirror at home.* I turn down to my girlfriend's face, imagining her smiling and giving me a thumbs-up. *"You got this, babe."*

Inhale. Exhale. "I never thought I would be strong enough to do this—to confront you after everything that's happened." They stare at me in surprise, expectantly waiting. "I'm not here to condemn you—or burden you with bad news—I'm just...tired of avoiding what needs to be done." I hold my breath and observe their faces, expecting the worst.

Helen turns to her husband with sullen eyes— softened after years of contemplation.

He takes her hand and pats it. "I think it's time, dear."

She nods and turns to me with a guilty expression. "We've been thinking this over for...a while. If you'll allow us, we'd like to try to reconcile. So, whatever you have to say—and I'm sure it's deserved—we're ready to hear it. We're ready for closure."

The flame in my chest flares and immediately dies back down. I let myself sit again.

I didn't think I would get this far.

"Okay. Say your piece; I'm ready to listen."

They explain their young ignorance and fears about their daughter's future, how they know they reacted poorly, and have since gained experience. They tell me how much they regretted their behavior once realizing that they might never be able to speak to her again. They admit they still don't completely understand but are willing to expand their horizons.

"Nothing can make up for our abhorrent actions, I know. But we want you to know that we have so much respect for how you've handled it all, how you've taken care of her," Frank admits.

"All we ever wanted was for her to be happy; that's why we left her alone after our fight. And because we were afraid of facing the consequences. I'm so glad you're here…so we can't run anymore. We're so sorry. We would give anything to take back what we did and start over… To tell her how we feel…" Helen is crying now.

I nod and realize I'm crying too. I'm surprised by their reaction—I didn't think they would be so…cooperative—but I understand; I'm human too.

It's time to let go.

I outstretch my arms and wrap them both in an awkward hug to try to express my empathy. "I can't speak for her, but I forgive you. I think she would want this to happen. She missed you."

They lightly hug back and wipe their eyes when we pull away.

Helen nods. "Oh, we miss her so much. I wish we'd been there for her before…the accident." She knows it was the Receiver's burden her child took, and she's clearly kept it secret from her husband.

"Yes, we'd give anything to spend time with her again. If only…" Frank trails off and leans against his wife, who holds him close.

I look over to Sleeping Beauty on the bed—positively serene, and lovelier than ever. I hope she heard everything; she needs this more than I do.

"Do you think–" I look up, my eyes stinging–"that there's still hope? That maybe…she'll wake up?" *I need her. I miss her.*

They slowly move to her side, Frank's hand on Helen's shoulder. Her lips quiver as she looks down at her daughter's blank face, reaching for her cheek with a shaky hand.

"Have you tried"—Helen cracks a small smile—"true love's kiss?" She strokes her daughter's cheek, the unmistakable sparkle of admiration in her eyes.

I take in a breath and wipe more tears away, chortling softly. "I have…but I don't think I'm what she needs this time." I sit in the chair on the other side of my girlfriend and hold her limp hand, my heart abnormally warm.

Helen nods. "You're right; we should have been there for her."

Frank replies meekly, "I just hope it's not too late."

Helen leans down, Frank's hand touching her back, and lays a kiss on her daughter's forehead. We peer upon her unchanging face in fear of all that we have to lose. I squeeze my girlfriend's hand.

She squeezes mine back. Then a fire ignites inside my chest and spreads throughout my limbs as I feel life awaken inside her. The monitor beeps faster as conscious breath inflates her lungs. Helen and Frank call for a doctor as I lean closer to my love.

The rest of the world goes silent and still as two lucid eyes open and shine their light on me. *She's awake!* My heart cries for my long-lost angel—finally found—as love pours out of my soul and into her gaze. My chest no longer burns.

"Oh, hi there," she gruffly mumbles, raising her eyebrows at me as if it's any other day.

I caress her face and grin in shock and euphoria. "It's about damn time." And then I crush my lips against hers.

We've already missed a year; I'm not wasting another second.

Her lips taste the same, if not somewhat bitter from her sleep. She holds me close and reminds me of who I am. When we release each other, I can see her smile and yearning eyes, while mine surely portray relief and ecstasy.

"You look *beautiful*," she breathes.

A thought strikes me. "You can see again!" I beam.

Now that she's no longer the Receiver, the only burdens she must bear are her own. So every pain and disability ever bestowed unto her are nonexistent now.

It worked.

She makes the slightest smirk. "What I miss?"

The doctors don't know how to explain it, but something stimulated enough brain activity to rouse her and the rest of her body—against all odds too. No complaints here; it's a goddamn miracle.

There's nothing I want more than to never stop kissing her, to make up for all our lost time. But alas, we're not alone just yet.

"Mom? Dad?" She's sitting up, still in bed—afraid to walk just yet—as she blinks up at her estranged parents, baffled. "What are you doing here?"

Frank squeezes Helen's hand and answers, "Something we should have done a long time ago."

She has some recollection of all the things she passively heard during her coma, but everything is in bits and pieces, like a dream. Now her parents are finally able to admit to her their mistakes. And they do. I notice Helen hold her breath as they wait for a response.

But my girlfriend just pulls them both into the biggest hug and squeezes them tight. "I've missed you." She smiles in sweet relief.

They reciprocate, equally elated. "We've missed you too."

When they finally let go, she takes my hand and yanks me onto her lap and into her tender embrace. "Don't think I've forgotten about you."

I wrap my arms around her neck and give her a long, loving kiss. "Never." *And I'm sure as hell not gonna let you.*

Helen and Frank blush awkwardly as my eyes land on them again.

"So," Helen begins, "you two will continue living together?"

"Yes, Mom, I've left her alone for far too long. Our apartment must be a mess by now."

I snicker at her tease. *She's not wrong.*

"But," she continues, "once we clean it up and get reacclimated, I guess we should have you over for dinner sometime." She smiles up at them; they're at a loss for words.

I guess it really was about forgiveness.

And her parents tear up again, but out of joy this time.

"Mom, do you remember when I was younger and you used to tell me that one day I wouldn't think boys were gross anymore?" She pauses, and Helen tilts her head. "Well, you were wrong."

We all laugh—or snort, if you're me—genuinely for the first time in a long time.

I bet she was sleeping on that one.

The nurses all insist she stay in the hospital another night for close monitoring, but the second they let me, we practically run out of there.

"What's for dinner tonight?" My girlfriend utters through a mouthful of the last of the "I forgive you" crescent rolls I made—and then forgot in the car, overnight.

Luckily, I snag one before she can finish them off. "Seriously, babe? I mean, I know it's been a year without eating through your mouth, but...you also ate my emergency beef jerky!" I exclaim.

She shrugs.

I turn to her after parking in front of our building, and melt in the warmth of her sweet smile. "Alright, I'll make something special, just for you."

She stops me before I get out. "For us."

I lean toward her. "For us."

Then we close the gap.

"Welcome home."

I open and close the door behind us as she takes it all in. Not much has changed, except it looks kind of sad without her art on the walls.

We can fix that.

I toss an arm around her neck as I gesture to the—only mildly—cluttered space. "See, angel? Not a total mess."

And then I see tears begin to trail down her face. "So many things are different. You're almost done with college…Beyoncé is having twins… How am I supposed to catch up?"

I turn to her and hold her shoulders steadily. "With help, of course." I tuck a piece of hair behind her ear. "Gosh, you need a haircut."

We laugh through our tears.

Her eyes flicker like a light. "Oh! I almost forgot—what's your, um, ailment today?"

"Oh, I guess I forgot too. I don't know…" I shrug. "Heartburn? Or was that yesterday?" I chuckle softly, knowing it was much deeper than that—like some burning passion I could finally release. *Whatever it was, it's not important; she's home.* "Anyway, pasta and Alfredo sauce?"

After we eat, I notice how quiet she's been. "Overwhelming, huh?" I grasp her hand from across the table.

She looks up from her empty plate to me. "Uh, yeah, actually."

"Why don't we have some ice cream then?" *Ice cream always makes her feel better.*

I begin to stand, but she tightens her grip on me. "No, wait."

I'm shocked. "No? To dessert? Wow, that coma sure did a number on you."

She glowers at me, annoyed.

"Sorry. Honey, are you okay?"

"What? Yes. Shut up!" she barks, releasing my hand.

Taking a breath, she moves her chair closer to my side of the table and offers both hands to me. I take them.

"I'm sorry, it's just… Beautiful, you've grown so much since we first met—hell, even in the past year. You let a grudge go, *against my parents*, and I am so grateful for that." She smiles warmly.

I give a shy smile back. "I know how important your relationship with them is."

"And you care! You've always cared so much, about… damn near everything. I remember some of your rants."

She laughs. "I'm just sorry you had to rant alone, but you don't now. I…used to wait, and just hope for the best. You taught me—taught me how to take initiative, go after what you want. And I know what I want."

What's happening here? I must be dreaming. But I can't pinch myself to check, since she has my hands. *I'd better not cry again.*

"If there's one thing that that coma taught me, it's that I can't wait anymore."

She moves her chair back with her foot as she gets down on one knee before me. I choke back a sob as she continues.

"I want to grow and learn and change with you. I want to destroy the patriarchy with you. But most importantly, I just want to *be* with you, for as long as you'll have me. I don't have a ring—and I know you think they're arbitrary symbols of outdated traditions and we wouldn't need them to show our loyalty to each other—but…" She inhales sharply, eyes sparkling with sheer love and hope. "Will you marry me anyway?"

I take a deep breath, savoring the moment as I gaze down at her ethereal face.

"Oh, angel."

A (second) fresh start would be nice.

EPILOGUE

Love is Love

Ten years later...

"Babe! We're running low on celery; mind making a run?" I'm making egg salad sandwiches for the annual community picnic, or I'm at least going to try.

"On it, beautiful. I just know that they're going to be the pinnacle of your neighborhood mom reputation," my angel mocks, kissing my cheek in the process. *That scoundrel.*

I had always hoped we would get here; I just didn't know how we would do it. Frankly, I didn't quite believe it would happen. But she pushed me forward—kept me going all these years, along with the vexing desire to remain existing solely out of spite.

Regardless, here we are—all five of us. Not long after her...extended nap...came to an end, my girlfriend became my fiancée. We were tired of waiting for forever to begin.

My ring glimmers in contrast to the half balls of watermelon I'm butchering. *Maybe I'll stick to slices.*

The wedding happened a year later. We looked smashing. It was small; there were more flowers than people—like, a *lot* more. My partner really outdid herself. Oh yes, she arranged most of it. Turns out she has a real knack for event planning. Who knew? (I knew.)

"I'm serious, angel! This is my mom's recipe, and I wanna get it right." I turn back to my gorgeous wife leaning against the kitchen counter, about to eat one of my hard-boiled eggs.

She makes eye contact and slowly returns the egg with the others in the fridge. "Okay, do you want me to get you a proper melon-baller as well?"

I scowl, putting down the weird scooper thing.

I could go on for an eternity talking about just the ceremony—her gown alone would take me ages... I'll spare you the details, but there is one thing I'll mention: over my dress, I wore the snazziest black tuxedo blazer; she nearly swooned.

At this moment, a couple of chalk-covered gremlins barge through the kitchen door and scamper around the island, one bumping into my wife and the other into me. *Thank goodness for jeans.*

I guess I should mention the kids. There are two of them; we adopted. First there was Harper, who's four now, and a bouncy little one too. Then Riley, who we met later; the once apprehensive seven-year-old is really starting to make a home with us here. I'm ecstatic. They keep each other company—playing together when we're too busy working, but we're insistent on family game night once a week. I crush them at Trivial Pursuit, the wife always wins Uno, and the kids somehow always beat us at Jenga. I think Harper cheats.

There's never a dull moment, that's for sure. When we can't take them with us on work trips, they stay with either my mom or my parents-in-law. I wish they could've met Grandma Ruth; she would've loved them, and vice versa.

The funeral was extravagant; I think she would've approved. My wife never thought it was enough. She held my hand the whole time. I told her, "She will always live in our hearts." She almost laughed at that; it may have been corny, but it was true.

"Hey, what did I tell you guys? Brush your hands off *before* you touch things—and me." My wife shakes her head at the new orange handprints on her sundress.

I snicker. "Who wants to go shopping with Mommy, and who wants to help Momma with the picnic food…?" I propose hopefully.

Riley tugs on my darling's sundress. "I wanna go shopping."

Harper raises a hand toward me, then reaches past me for a melon half ball. *That'll do.*

Oscar always misses us when we go off to rallies, or the grocery store, or anywhere he can't see us, actually. We can tell he misses us because once we sit down, he plops onto our laps and won't let us get back up. Right now he's probably cozy in the living room, with the couch all to himself. The kids are usually gentle, but he still likes to avoid the ruckus.

He's a cat, by the way—black and white, always seems like he's up to something. I picked him up at the shelter. My wife was overjoyed, or aggravated; either way, her eyes were watering. Turns out she was allergic. My bad. Luckily, she adjusted over time and grew a higher tolerance for him. Thank goodness, because neither of us had the heart to return him. But my *god* is he noisy. He talks nonstop—about who knows what. I love him, but a girl needs her sleep.

Well, at least a bit of sleep, when we aren't, *you know…* taking down the patriarchy. Did I mention that I minored in women's and gender studies? I'm a reporter now; I focus mainly on social dilemmas and try to highlight every local activist affair—which my fabulous wife generally organizes, as a canvass director for the Equality Fund. She's quite proud of that title. (I am too, but it's fun to tease her about it.)

"Oh yeah, you got that article out yet about the thing?" she asks, distracted by the large toddler that's now on her hip (with *my* watermelon).

"You mean the protest outside of city council over the local women's health center? That thing?"

She cleans off Harper's hands and nods. "Yeah, I've got dozens of flyers to hand out at the picnic. Since only so many people can fit in the building, we'll need the outside support."

I smile, thinking of the graphically pleasing flyers she designed herself. I'm so proud of her.

Together we get the word out. We are advocates for change. Be it LGBTQ+, Black Lives Matter, other people of color, the disabled, the neurodivergent, the old or young, the skinny or fat—anyone who doesn't fit the default, acceptable standards of society—we defend them and their right to be themselves.

I set the lumps of watermelon aside for Riley or whoever gets to them first.

"Who run the world?" I call.

On cue, both kids cry, "Girls!"

Which they are, but it's really fun to ignore the confines of gender and use neutral pronouns until they each discover their identities for themselves. I also figured out that I don't particularly care about gender either and have played around with she/her and they/them pronouns for myself, which is cool. Anyway, you should've seen the looks on our neighbors' faces during the adoption shower (it's a new thing)—rainbow confetti everywhere. My wife and I joked, "It's a gay!" I still laugh about it. We don't want our children to think they have to fit a certain parameter or stereotype; they just are. And what they are is happy. The carefree smiles on their faces are enough.

When We Rise sparked the flame in my heart into a blazing wildfire, and now I can't stop. I don't want to stop. My partner and I have such great purpose. Receiver matters aside, the world is still moving around us, and we're not gonna wait for it to slow down.

That's another thing: I decided—*we* decided—that it would be best for the world if the legend ended with us, with me. Which is why we adopted. That and we didn't want to go through the whole sperm-donor thing. And who has time to be pregnant anyway? In this economy?? I already almost missed my sister's (second) wedding because of the bizarre curse; nobody likes a bridesmaid with barf-breath.

The picnic is bustling and noisy, full of familiar faces and the smell of hotdogs cooking. So we release the hounds and let them play with the other kids, watching them out of the corners of our eyes. I set up the dishes we brought as she passes out her flyers, talking it up with the other moms.

But before she gets too far, we spot some familiar faces. My mother waves with a big smile of what I can only describe as relief. Then I notice my parents-in-law waving awkwardly next to her. *Ah, that's why.*

I take my wife's hand, and she turns, looking happily surprised to see them. "Mom! Dad! I didn't think you'd come. Hi, Momma, nice to see you." She hugs my mom first.

"Yes, well," Helen answers, "we decided to cut our ski trip short."

She and Frank hug her tightly.

"Family is more important," Frank explains.

Helen whispers to her, "And your father is getting old."

I chuckle as my mother comes over to me, squishing me in a big bear hug. "Thank goodness you're here, hon; those two are so white I had to squint just to look at 'em."

I snort. "I've missed you, Momma."

"Now where are those grandkids of ours? That's the real reason we're here!" my mother (probably) jokes.

We point our parents in the direction of the random screaming off in the grass.

What an unexpected twist of fate.

My wife smiles and shakes her head as our parents walk off. "Thank you."

I turn to her, tilting my head. "For what?"

She bumps me with her hip. "For bringing them back into my life; I know it wasn't easy."

"Aw, baby"—I kiss her cheek—"you thanked me ten years ago, and that was more than enough."

She starts to say something but surrenders instead, touching my face and pulling it toward hers. *Even after all these years, she's still the one.*

After a minute, I playfully shove her away, shooing her to get to work on her canvassing. This place could use her initiative.

It's a pretty diverse community, but there's only so much we citizens can do on our own. That's what organizing is for. We get people who care involved with the issues of the community and the country.

I smile and snag some cookies, pretending my head isn't suddenly on fire.

Stupid curse. I wonder if it's like a period; maybe one day I'll go through Receiver menopause and then it'll go away. The good thing about all these feelings is that mine tend to overpower those of the bestowers. Gotta love that eternal rage of a thousand suns. Anyway, I'm just glad my kids won't have to deal with this supernatural crap on top of all the other crap. I guess the world will just have to deal with its own crap problems from now on. No one person should have to take on such a burden. Which reminds me…

I'm basically stuck with this curse until I die, so I'm self-employed. I started a blog and everything. However—I realize at my age—blogs don't connect so much with teens anymore. Damn Cyber Era. At least memes will never die. I write articles on my small website, working with some other equally angry millennials. Of course, we aren't the younger generation anymore, but I think we do our best to make things better for the upcoming generation of terrified adults.

Suddenly people are talking to me. "Hey! Oh my gosh, I *loved* your take on the worldwide green movement, how 'after China's mistakes, they're becoming the role model America should take after.' *So* inspiring." A young brunette starts gushing about her new garden and how it somehow compares to China's man-made forests.

"And your piece on Warren's memorial—I teared up. You're right; she was *such* a political hero for our generation." A blond guy I don't recognize sips his iced tea at me.

I look back and forth between them, speechless. *I don't think he read the whole article.* "Wow, um, thanks. Are you guys…local?" *Where are my awkward parents-in-law when I need them?*

The two nod, then shake their heads, and then tilt them.

The woman replies, "Kind of. We're around the block for half the year. The—"

The man interrupts. "The rest of the year we're in Morocco, helping out."

The girl jumps back in. "We bring them fresh water. You know, to Africa." They nod diplomatically.

I smile and nod back. "Oh *yeah*, that's—*wow*." I snag a flyer off of my wife's distracted person and hold it out to them. "If you guys care so much, you should really attend our local protest next weekend. The wife and a few *girlfriends* of ours are gonna sit in while the rest of us inform the people of how helpful the women's shelter is." I always use "girlfriend" ironically—well, now that I'm married at least. Before that, it would have been very confusing.

The two exchange glances and hesitantly take the flyer. They say they'll consider it and walk off. *Phew.* I'll probably never see them again.

My unnatural headache subsides (for now), so I take my cookies and wander over to the kids. They're much more interesting than the adults—besides my mother, who's probably off getting some recipe from my neighbors, and, of course, my wife. She's off with the Miltons, ranting their ears off. But unlike some, they seem to actually give a damn about what she's talking about.

I take a seat by the other parents on duty and overhear Riley teaching the Jeffersons' sons—try saying that ten times fast—that girls are just as capable as boys and that "like a girl" shouldn't be synonymous with "weak." I couldn't be prouder.

I can't wait to gush about this to my honey later, with Oscar in my lap. Maybe we'll all rewatch some *Doctor Who* together—probably the seasons with thirteen, the first female Doctor; the kids love her almost as much as I do. Then I and my favorite person will make out for a while with some old Haley Kiyoko songs blaring in the background so the kids don't hear us. We haven't forgotten to lock the door for a while now…hopefully we won't make that mistake again.

Speak of the angel. My wife takes a seat on the bench beside me. "Hey beautiful, I've got half a dozen flyers left; you think the other kids would show them to their parents?"

I wrap my arm around her waist and let her head rest on my shoulder. "Let's find out." I whistle at the munchkins, summoning Harper and Riley, and show them the flyers. "This is your mission, should you choose to accept it." They giggle before I ask them to hand the papers out to their grandparents and their friends—even the ones that aren't their friends, because you never know.

They take the flyers and run off, doing God's work (so to speak, unless God really is a woman).

My lady lover chuckles. "Let's get some grub, director, before the agents return."

We entwine our fingers together, standing up with the intention of taking more food than our stomachs can handle.

Our love burns like a mother—or two, raising their kids while taking on the world. And it will never stop. But it's not the only thing.

This rage burns deep inside my core, like a blazing inferno just waiting to be uncaged. But this—this is a rage I've carried for centuries within my soul. I feel the weight of it; it's ancient, powerful, and it can render me frozen inside my own wrath if I let it. But with her loving hand in mine, I can soar.

We are the girls that feel—misery, fear, and, above all, compassion. Before, we just felt, but now we have direction.

Now, we bestow our wisdom unto the world.

P.S. The egg salad turned out pretty tasty.

Printed in the United States
By Bookmasters